This
Gormiti Annual
belongs to

_____

Age _____

My favourite Gormiti is

_____

GORMITI
The Lords of Nature Return!

ANNUAL 2011

EGMONT
We bring stories to life

First published in Great Britain in 2010 by Egmont UK Limited
239 Kensington High Street, London W8 6SA
Gormiti Series and Images from the Series:
© 2010 Giochi Preziosi S.p.A and Marathon
and all related logos, names and distinctive likenesses are the exclusive
property of GIOCHI PREZIOSI and MARATHON. All rights reserved.
Inspired by Leandro Consumi's original work "Gormiti"
Text © 2010 Egmont UK Limited
Written by Jenny Bak. Designed by Andrea Pollock.

ISBN 978 1 4052 5409 0
3 5 7 9 10 8 6 4 2
Printed in Italy

CONTENTS

Elemental Powers Flow ...
Gormiti Lords of Nature
GO!

Ever wondered what it would be like to have super powers? Nick, Toby, Jessica and Lucas don't have to wonder - they've got 'em!

Join the Lords of Nature in their mission to defend Gorm from the dark forces of the Volcano Gormiti, and save planet Earth from destruction as well!

This annual is packed with cool activities, tricky puzzles and awesome stories, plus all the important facts about the amazing world of Gormiti!

The Origins of Gorm

For as long as anyone could remember, the island of Gorm was inhabited by peaceful creatures called Gormiti. They lived in nations that were connected to each element of nature – Sea, Air, Forest and Earth. These nations, made of many small tribes, lived in great harmony with each other.

Looming above Gorm was

a volcano known as Fire Mountain. One fateful day, the volcano erupted, destroying the peace and harmony of Gorm forever!

During the eruption, the Gormiti saw fiery creatures rising from the flowing lava. These new Gormiti formed the Volcano Nation and began a fierce war against the others. Their only wish was to conquer Gorm!

There seemed to be no hope that peace would return to Gorm, until one day, when four unexpected heroes arrived ...

Welcome to Venture Falls, the quiet town that's home to Nick and Toby Tripp, along with their friends, Lucas and Jessica. The Tripp family's house may seem ordinary, but it's hiding a big secret. Under the kitchen and down a secret passageway is the Primal Pad, filled with strange books, glowing crystals and a portal to Gorm called the Gorm Gate!

Can you find Razzle hiding in the picture?

Answer on page 68.

Portal Power

The Volcano Gormiti are on the attack! Help the team jump through the portal and head to the Forest Nation to help the Forest Gormiti defend their tribe.

START

OUT

IN

FINISH

Answers on page 68.

Super Search

Magmion, one of the Volcano Nation's leaders, is on the move! Cross out the words as you find them in the grid below. When you've finished, unscramble the letters in the yellow boxes to find out who he's attacking next.

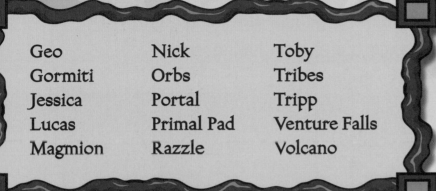

Geo	Nick	Toby
Gormiti	Orbs	Tribes
Jessica	Portal	Tripp
Lucas	Primal Pad	Venture Falls
Magmion	Razzle	Volcano

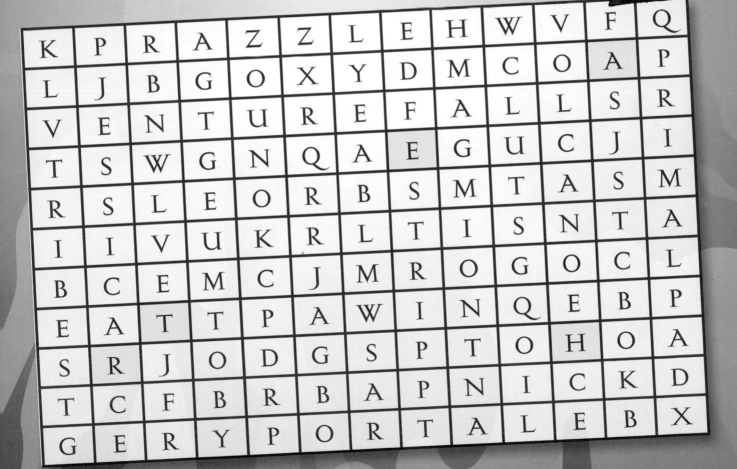

K	P	R	A	Z	Z	L	E	H	W	V	F	Q
L	J	B	G	O	X	Y	D	M	C	O	A	P
V	E	N	T	U	R	E	F	A	L	L	S	R
T	S	W	G	N	Q	A	E	G	U	C	J	I
R	S	L	E	O	R	B	S	M	T	A	S	M
I	I	V	U	K	R	L	T	I	S	N	T	A
B	C	E	M	C	J	M	R	O	G	O	C	L
E	A	T	T	P	A	W	I	N	Q	E	B	P
S	R	J	O	D	G	S	P	T	O	H	O	A
T	C	F	B	R	B	A	P	N	I	C	K	D
G	E	R	Y	P	O	R	T	A	L	E	B	X

Magmion is attacking the _____ Nation.

POWERS OF THE SEA

Toby

AGE: 13 YEARS OLD

PERSONALITY: ROUGH AND TUMBLE

FUN FACT: LIKES PULLING PRANKS

FLAWS: IMPULSIVE

Lord of Sea

POWERS: HE CAN BLAST WATER GLOBES FROM HIS BODY

HIS HAIR BECOMES STRONG TENTACLES

HIS ARM TRANSFORMS INTO A GIANT CLAW

HE CAN CONTROL WATER WITH HIS MIND

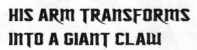

HE'S QUICK AND NIMBLE, ESPECIALLY IN WATER

WEAKNESS: IF TOBY GETS TOO HOT, HIS POWERS EVAPORATE LIKE STEAM

The team quickly transforms into the Lords of Nature ...

Elemental Powers Flow ...
Gormiti Lords of Nature – GO!

Take THAT, lava-eater!

WRRIP!

ARGHHH!

Toby's tidal wave crashes over the villains and washes them away!

Steelback, why were those uglies attacking you?

It's all because of the Sulphur Stone ...

Lavor and Screaming Guardian stole our Sulphur Stone, which contains great power. Now they're back to capture the Earth Gormiti. With the stone as their weapon, no one can stop them!

We'll see about that!

Suddenly, a raging storm floods the Rocklands, weakening the river dam!

Must not ... let go ...

Water? That's my turf!

WHOOSH!

As Toby holds back the flood, Nick pulls a huge slab of stone from the ground to make a new dam!

Unnghhh!

CRACK!

Lucas, the storm is coming from that mountain. What is it?

Bad news. That's Boulder Peak. The book says there's a cosmic opening between Earth and Gorm at the very top.

The Volcano Gormiti are using the Sulphur Stone to destroy your world and ours!

The heroes speed to Boulder Peak to stop the Volcano Gormiti, but they're too late. The Sulphur Stone has reached its full power!

Toby launches an attack ...

Sea Gormiti

THE SEA GORMITI ARE AS FAST AND MYSTERIOUS AS THE FISH IN THE OCEAN.

MY FAVOURITE SEA GORMITI IS

_____

Jelly Fish

Quarry

22

Helico

Mantra

Delos

Crabs

Tongs

Turtle the Seer

Hammer

Sea Soldier

23

Power Puzzles

One of these pictures of Toby is different from the rest.
Can you spot the odd one out?

How many of the smaller Sea Orbs match the big orb?

Answers on page 68.

Primal Code

The team is on a mission in Gorm with Nick as Keeper. He's found out the name of one of the Volcano Tribe's evil leaders. Use Nick's code below to fill in the blanks and reveal the name.

A   I   L   N   O   V

His name is _____.

Nick

AGE: 12 YEARS OLD

PERSONALITY: CURIOUS

FUN FACT: CAN'T KEEP A SECRET

FLAWS: HE'S A KNOW-IT-ALL

Lord of Earth

POWERS: HE SHOOTS ROCKS FROM HIS ARM

HE PUNCHES THE GROUND TO MAKE THE EARTH SHAKE

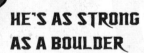

HE'S AS STRONG AS A BOULDER

HIS HANDS TRANSFORM INTO HAMMERS OR DRILLS

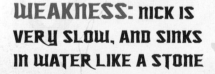

WEAKNESS: NICK IS VERY SLOW, AND SINKS IN WATER LIKE A STONE

Going Green

A typical day at Venture Falls Junior High School ...

Hey, this is my shortcut home!

Not any more. It's also home to the rare Venture Falls Speckled Sparrow.

Take the long way, it's good for your health!

But Ike goes through anyway, almost stepping on a sparrow. Lucas saves it in the nick of time!

Got it!

That was a close one!

Woah, where did you come from?

Bombos the Firepower is burning up the Forest Nation. Now fires are breaking out in Venture Falls, too.

Primal Pad, here we come!

Take this, fishface!

FWOOSH!

Toby spots a nearby stream ...

You could use a little mouthwash!

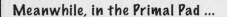

Meanwhile, in the Primal Pad ...

Lavaman? Lavatory? Lavion – got it!

Guys, this book says that Lavion was banished for a hundred years by a Forest Gormiti using scroll magic!

That Gormiti must have been Mimic!

Unggh ... Mimic, banish him again!

N-no! I can't go through that again!

WHAT?

Never fear, a Forest Gormiti is here. I'll read the scroll!

Forest magic, Trees and seeds ...

Open a portal To suit my needs!

The portal quickly sucks in Lavion and Bombos, then closes back up. The forest is safe! But Mimic flees the scene before the boys can question him.

Lucas, are you OK?

I think so. I wonder why Mimic didn't want to read the scroll? Hmm ...

At school the next day ...

Hey Lucas! That's a cool new look!

Look? What look?

All day at school, leaves and bark continue to grow on Lucas. He gives Ike the scare of his life!

Ahhhh! Tree freak! I'll never hurt nature again, I promise!

The team holds an emergency meeting at the Primal Pad.

Here's Lucas's problem – the Forest orb! Some of its glow got trapped in Lavion's portal.

You need to take the orb into the portal to get back all its glow!

Back in Destiny Valley ...

Lucas, are you sure you want to read the scroll again?

Beware, friends. I read that scroll a hundred years ago and also turned into a tree. I still have not regained my strength.

But before Lucas can answer, bark grows over his body ... and his mouth!

One of us will have to read it now!

No. I will read the scroll, as I should have done in the first place.

Mimic opens up the portal, to the surprise of Lavion and Bombos.

Wha-!

Toby and Nick quickly transform ...

Look, the orb's getting back its missing glow!

But Lavion snatches the glowing orb with his massive claw hand!

This looks like it would be fun to crush!

THWOCK!

Not so fast, ugly!

With the orb fully restored, Nick and Toby jump back through the portal as Lavion lunges after them. His claw drives into the ground – and gets stuck!

Nooooooo! Don't leave us here!

Back in Destiny Valley ...

It's working! Lucas is turning back to normal!

It's working on Mimic too!

I feel like a young Gormiti again. Thank you, friends.

And at school, there's been another transformation ...

Never hurt nature ... never hurt nature ...

THE END

34

Double Dare

Draw over the lines to finish the picture, then colour it in.

The Primal Pad

The Primal Pad is where Toby, Jessica, Lucas and Nick start their missions. Powered by magical crystals, the Pad's control centre lets one member of the team – the Keeper – guide the team through sticky situations.

The power orbs control the team's amazing abilities. Once Nick, Toby, Jessica and Lucas jump through the portal to Gorm, their orbs fill up with energy and the heroes are able to transform into the powerful Lords of Nature. But when the orbs run out of energy, the Lords' powers run out, too!

MAGICAL BOOKS ON GORM

CONTROL CENTRE

THE GREAT BOOK OF GORM

Razzle

This lizard may look small, but he knows a lot about Gorm! Whenever a natural disaster happens in Venture Falls, Razzle knows that something's wrong in Gorm and summons the team to the Primal Pad straight away.

POWER ORBS

**GORM GATE –
PORTAL TO GORM**

Spot the Difference

These pictures look the same, but 5 things are different in picture 2. Can you spot them all?

Answers on page 68.

Earth Gormiti

THE EARTH GORMITI ARE STRONG AND GENEROUS BY NATURE.

Stone Thrower

Earth Eater

Earth Family

MY FAVOURITE EARTH GORMITI IS

_____

Bullrock

Jessica

AGE: 12 YEARS OLD

PERSONALITY: DREAMER

FUN FACT: LOVES TO SHOP

FLAWS: ABSENT-MINDED

Lord of Air

POWERS: SHE UNLEASHES STORMY WINDS

SHE THROWS FEATHER DARTS

SHE SHOOTS OUT POWER SPHERES

HER WINGS HAVE RAZOR EDGES

SHE'S FAST AND NIMBLE, ESPECIALLY IN THE AIR

WEAKNESS: JESSICA HAS TROUBLE USING HER POWERS UNDERGROUND OR IN SMALL SPACES

Air Gormiti

THE AIR GORMITI ARE AS QUICK AND AGILE AS BIRDS.

Extra Solitary Eagle

Solitary Eagle

Each of the photos at the top show a Gormiti nation - Sea, Air, Earth, Forest and Volcano. Write the name of the nation below each picture.

AIR

FOREST

MAP OF GORM

VOLCANO

SEA

EARTH

The Keeper Kept

There's trouble brewing at the Archaeology Club meeting ...

I started this club, Ike. That's why I'm president!

Not for long! The election's tonight, and I'm gonna WIN!

Nick is upset, but the others have something else to worry about ...

There is severe flooding in the subways and streets of Venture Falls. Officials say the seawater appeared out of thin air!

Guess I'd better come save the day!

Toby jumps into the portal and transforms into a Lord of Nature!

Power of the Sea!

But Firespitter commands Nick, Lucas and Jessica to destroy Toby!

Bro, snap out of it!

Toby splashes water on his friends and breaks the spell. But they're not out of danger yet!

Get them!

Jessica flies the team to a cave, where they find two Sea Gormiti hiding.

I am Mantra and that is Delos. We can tell you what Firespitter wants.

Firespitter sends a hypnotised Sea Gormiti to fight them, but the power in the heroes' orbs is fading fast!

WHIRRR!

WHIRRR!

Could the timing be any worse? My powers have gone!

Me too!

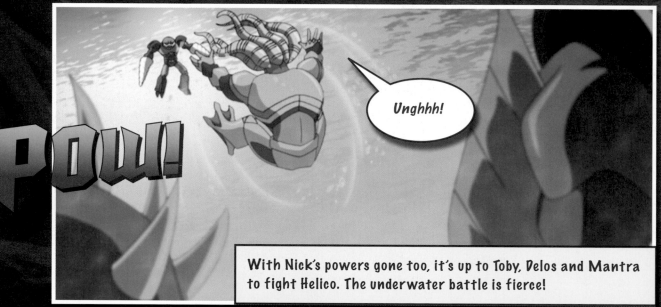

POW!

Unghhh!

With Nick's powers gone too, it's up to Toby, Delos and Mantra to fight Helico. The underwater battle is fierce!

As Toby's power runs out, Helico's drill hands dig up a curious object ...

Even without superpowers, the others use a seaweed lasso to give Firespitter and Crabs a cold bath in the sea!

It's the Lost Heart of Desire!

YANK!

Woahhhhh!

The Lords of Volcano

POWERFUL AND NASTY, THE VOLCANO GORMITI DON'T
GET ON WELL WITH ANYBODY, NOT EVEN EACH OTHER!

THE VOLCANO NATION HAS TWO LEADERS,
THE LORD OF MAGMA AND THE LORD OF LAVA:

Magmion – Lord of Magma

MAGMION IS THE MOST EVIL CREATURE THAT
EVER LIVED IN GORM! HIS ULTIMATE WISH IS
TO TAKE OVER THE WORLD AND MAKE THE
OTHER GORMITI HIS SLAVES.

Lavion – Lord of Lava

WITH CONTROL OVER MOLTEN LAVA AND
A POWERFUL CLAW HAND, LAVION IS A
DEADLY ENEMY. EXTREMELY SELFISH AND
VAIN, LAVION THINKS HIS ENEMIES SHOULD
FEEL HONOURED TO BE DEFEATED BY HIM!

Drakkon

AS THE ELEMENTAL GUARDIAN OF LAVA, DRAKKON IS A FIERCE DRAGON WHO SPITS LAVA. BY RIDING DRAKKON, MAGMION CAN TAKE HIS CAMPAIGN OF TERROR TO THE SKIES OF GORM!

Volcano Gormiti

THE VOLCANO GORMITI ARE FIERY AND DESTRUCTIVE, JUST LIKE MOLTEN LAVA!

MY FAVOURITE VOLCANO GORMITI IS

_____

Deepdown Fear

Firespitter

Lava Soldier

Lavor

Electricon

Screaming
Guardian

Bombos

53

Battle of the Boxes

The Lords of Nature are at war with the Volcano Nation!
Who will win — the good guys or the bad guys?

Play this game with a friend - choose to be Lord or Volcano.
Take it in turns to draw a line connecting any two dots.
The line can be up and down or straight across - no diagonals!
Try to form a four-sided box as shown below. The player who
completes the fourth side of the box writes L (for Lord) or
V (for Volcano) inside, then draws a new line. When all the
dots have been used, count up the Ls and Vs. The player with
the most boxes is the winner!

Ancient Guardians of Gorm

These magical beasts are as old as Gorm itself. Together with Drakkon, they are the elemental keepers of the land. They assist the Lords of Nature whenever they can.

Can you guess which element each Guardian belongs to – Sea, Air, Earth or Forest? Write it in! Hint: check which Lord of Nature is riding each Guardian.

Fenison,
Elemental Guardian of

_____

Roscalion,
Elemental Guardian of

_____

Troncalion,
Elemental Guardian of

_____

Tentaclion,
Elemental Guardian of

_____

Answers on page 68.

Lucas

AGE: 11 YEARS OLD

PERSONALITY: SUPPORTS THE UNDERDOG

FUN FACT: LIKES TELLING JOKES

FLAWS: CAN BE TOO FOCUSED ON ONE THING

POWERS OF THE FOREST

Lord of Forest

POWERS: HE CAN SHOOT OUT AND REGROW HIS WOODEN FIST

HIS BREATH PUTS OTHERS INTO A DEEP SLEEP

HE HAS CONTROL OVER PLANTS AND FOREST ANIMALS

HIS ARMS AND LEGS TRANSFORM INTO CREEPER VINES AND ROOTS

WEAKNESS: IF LUCAS STAYS TOO LONG IN A DRY PLACE, HIS POWERS BECOME WEAK

Hero Hunt

The Lords of Nature have beaten Magmion's forces in battle!
Write the numbers of the missing spaces next to the correct pieces.

Answers on page 68.

Forest Gormiti

THE FOREST GORMITI ARE AS TOUGH AND WISE AS THE TREES.

Florus the Poisoner

Cannon Trunk

The Thug

Lethalwip

Sporus the Terrible

Mimic

MY FAVOURITE FOREST GORMITI IS

_____

The Root of Evil

It's Mrs. Tripp's birthday, and Jessica and Lucas are helping Nick and Toby set up a surprise party ...

So what kind of disaster are you giving Mum for a present this year, Toby?

Let's see, one year you gave her the psycho-kitty ...

And you can't forget the goldfish that didn't survive the day ...

Then the single used sock ...

I hate to interrupt, but you must go to Gorm right away!

Lavion and Bombos are back! They're feeding wood into a volcano to help it erupt. It will destroy the Forest nation if you don't stop them!

With Jessica as Keeper, the team is ready for action!

Let's go!

The Volcano Gormiti aren't happy to see the new arrivals.

ROAR!

Bombos shoots a ring of flame at Nick, who blasts back a whirlwind of stone!

SWIRR!

Meanwhile, Lucas struggles to escape Lavion's lava flow.

Woah!

CRACKLE!

I've got you now, weakling!

But Lavion is suddenly pelted by more rocks by a strange Forest Gormiti ...

Hyah!

Thanks to Cannon Trunk, the villains are driven back for the moment.

Thanks for saving my skin.

That was an awesome trick!

The honour is mine. I'm grateful to you for saving our forest.

If you're done with the pleasantries, I'd like to finish destroying you!

I have a plan, but all four of us have to work together!

Let's do it!

Here I come, lava loons!

Cannon Trunk shoots rock projectiles, stopping Lavion and Bombos in their tracks!

THWIPP!

THWIPP!

Nick picks up a rock and aims it at the lava, creating a huge molten splash.

Eat rock!

With Lavion and Bombos covered in lava, Toby blasts out ice-cold water spheres!

Time for you hotheads to COOL OFF!

THWOCK!

THWOCK!

63

Arrghhh!

Unngh!

SSSSSSS!

With the lava cooled into rock-hard stone, the evil villains are trapped!

It worked! The forest is saved!

All right!

We did it!

Nice teamwork!

Woah, look at this flower! It's a way better present than the toenail clippers I got for Mum!

After thanking Cannon Trunk, the team returns to Earth just in time ...

Surprise!

Then, suddenly ...

Yikes, this flower's trying to eat me! And it's growing!

He tosses it out the window, but Jessica notices a problem ...

Er, guys?

You're going back to Gorm and fixing this RIGHT NOW. I'll distract everyone as long as I can!

Back in Gorm, the team asks their forest friend for advice ...

There it is — that killer flower's going bye-bye!

You must find the flower's original root and destroy it. Only then will the flower shrink down.

STOMP! STOMP!

Later, back at the house ...

Toenail clippers! How did you know I needed them for your father's gnarly toenails! Thank you, dear, it's the perfect present.

Hee, hee!

THE END

Big Battle

Magmion is planning his biggest attack yet! Only the
Lords of Nature can save Gorm, and the Earth as well.
The first player to capture Magmion wins.
Let the Big Battle begin!

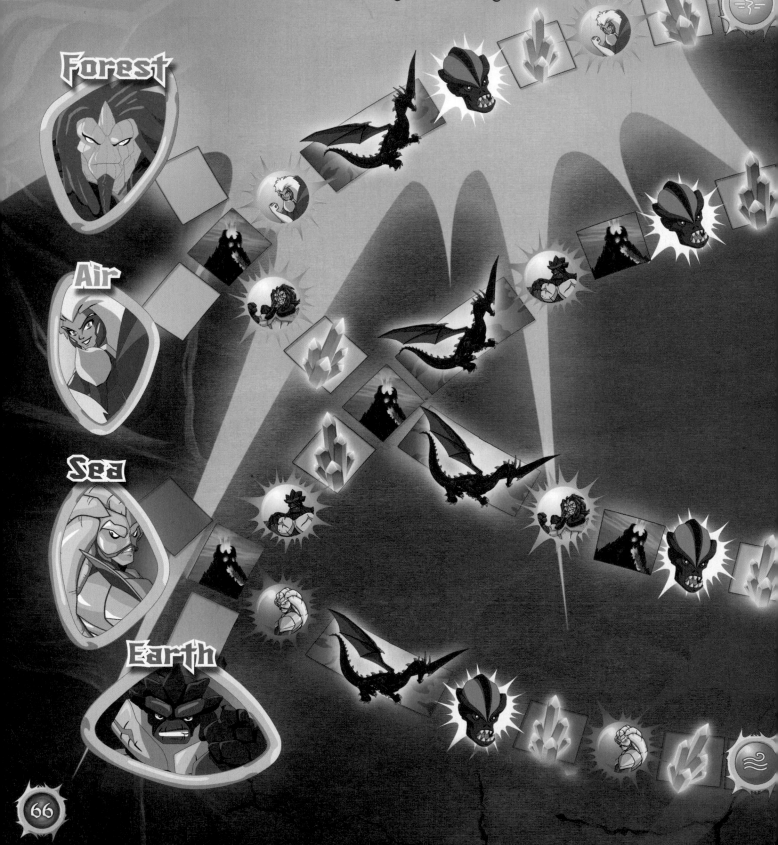

You will need:
A dice and counters (such as Gormiti toys) for up to four players.

How to play:
Decide which Lord of Nature each player will be, then place your counter on
your Lord picture on the left. Take it in turns to roll the dice and move along
your Lord's route. Follow the instructions for each space.
The first player to capture Magmion wins!

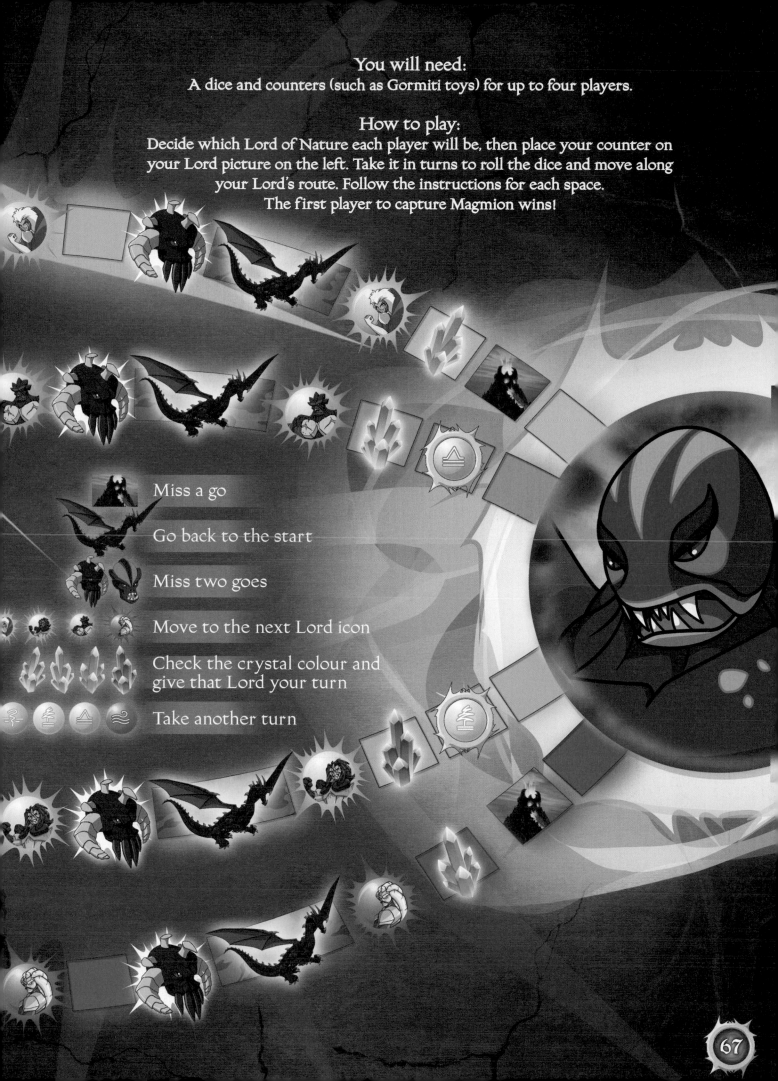

Miss a go

Go back to the start

Miss two goes

Move to the next Lord icon

Check the crystal colour and
give that Lord your turn

Take another turn

ANSWERS

10-11 Venture Falls
Razzle is hiding behind a tree to the right of the house.

12 Portal Power

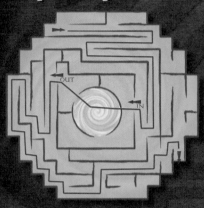

13 Super Search
Magmion is attacking the Earth Nation.

K	P	R	A	Z	Z	L	E	H	W	V	F	Q
L	I	B	G	O	X	Y	D	M	C	O	A	P
V	E	N	T	U	R	E	F	A	L	L	S	R
T	S	W	O	N	Q	A	E	G	U	C	J	J
R	S	L	E	O	R	B	S	M	T	A	S	M
I	I	V	U	K	R	L	T	S	N	T	A	A
B	C	E	M	C	J	M	R	O	G	O	C	L
E	A	T	T	P	A	W	I	N	Q	E	B	P
S	R	J	O	D	G	S	P	T	O	H	Q	A
T	C	F	B	R	B	A	P	N	I	C	K	D
G	E	R	Y	P	O	R	T	A	L	E	B	X

24 Power Puzzles
Picture 3 is the odd one out - Toby's middle is yellow.
Two orbs match the bigger one.

25 Primal Code
The leader's name is Lavion.

38 Spot the Difference

43 Map of Gorm
1. Volcano, 2. Air, 3. Earth, 4. Forest, 5. Sea

55 The Ancient Guardians of Gorm
Fenison - Air
Roscalion - Earth
Troncalion - Forest
Tentaclion - Sea

58 Hero Hunt